Miss Smith
Under the Ocean

SCHOOL BUS

MICHAEL GARLAND

DUTTON CHILDREN'S BOOKS ▪ *An imprint of Penguin Group (USA) Inc.*

DUTTON CHILDREN'S BOOKS • *A division of Penguin Young Readers Group*

PUBLISHED BY THE PENGUIN GROUP

Penguin Group (USA) Inc., 375 Hudson Street, New York, New York 10014, U.S.A. • Penguin Group (Canada), 90 Eglinton Avenue East, Suite 700, Toronto, Ontario M4P 2Y3, Canada (a division of Pearson Penguin Canada Inc.) • Penguin Books Ltd, 80 Strand, London WC2R 0RL, England • Penguin Ireland, 25 St Stephen's Green, Dublin 2, Ireland (a division of Penguin Books Ltd) • Penguin Group (Australia), 250 Camberwell Road, Camberwell, Victoria 3124, Australia (a division of Pearson Australia Group Pty Ltd) • Penguin Books India Pvt Ltd, 11 Community Centre, Panchsheel Park, New Delhi - 110 017, India • Penguin Group (NZ), 67 Apollo Drive, Rosedale, North Shore 0632, New Zealand (a division of Pearson New Zealand Ltd) • Penguin Books (South Africa) (Pty) Ltd, 24 Sturdee Avenue, Rosebank, Johannesburg 2196, South Africa • Penguin Books Ltd, Registered Offices: 80 Strand, London WC2R 0RL, England

Copyright © 2011 by Michael Garland

Published in the United States by Dutton Children's Books,
a division of Penguin Young Readers Group
345 Hudson Street, New York, New York 10014
www.penguin.com/youngreaders

Designed by Jason Henry
Manufactured in China • First Edition

ISBN: 978-0-525-42342-3
3 5 7 9 10 8 6 4 2

To all the fish in the sea

"**W**ell, class, I hope you all enjoy today's trip to the aquarium," Miss Smith said to her students after they got off the bus at their destination.

"Much of the earth is covered by water, and it is home to all kinds of plant and animal life. Today we are going to read from some wonderful stories that take place on the high seas," said Miss Smith, opening her book and starting to read.

Zack really loved hearing his teacher, Miss Smith, read from her *Incredible Storybook*. Whenever she read from the book, the stories actually came alive.

Miss Smith's first words were . . . "The Owl and the Pussycat went to sea in a beautiful pea-green boat . . . "

In an instant, Miss Smith and the whole class were crowded into the little green boat with the Owl and the Pussycat, bobbing up and down in the waves, far from any shore.

The Owl and the Pussycat looked surprised to see so many people with them. But Miss Smith didn't miss a beat! She opened her book and started to read again, but this time she read from *Moby Dick*. Just then, a huge white whale lunged out of the water and splashed down next to their boat, nearly capsizing them.

When the boat finally finished rocking, Sue-Ann asked Miss Smith if she would read her favorite story, "The Little Mermaid." No sooner had she started to read than Zack spotted a fish tail flopping in the water.

The class could see that it was the Little Mermaid herself, but she was tangled in a castaway fishnet.

"We have to save her!" shouted Zack.

The Pussycat quickly steered the pea-green boat to one side of the twisted net, then some of the class reached over and grabbed it so the Little Mermaid could get free.

"Oh, thank you," said the mermaid, after she was pulled up into the boat.

"You're just in time for a story," Miss Smith said to the Little Mermaid.

"Oh, goodie, I love pirate tales!" answered the mermaid.

Miss Smith started to read *Treasure Island* and sure enough, a short distance away everyone saw a pirate ship. It was stranded high and dry on a big rock that stuck out of the water.

The little green boat carefully approached the grounded ship.

"Ahoy there! Anybody home?" shouted Miss Smith.

"Ahoy yourself! We're home all right. And we're stuck, too," said Captain Long John Silver as he leaned over the rail with the rest of his cranky crew of pirates.

"Can we help?" Zack asked.

Long John Silver replied. "Yes, you can. We were searching for the island where we buried our treasure, when we ran aground. Can you mateys give us a ride?"

Without even waiting for an answer, the pirates climbed down from their

"There's an island close by," said the Little Mermaid. "Maybe that's where you buried your treasure." So they headed there while Derrick took the book and started to read from a story called *Robinson Crusoe*.

When they reached the beach, a very happy man dressed in ragged clothes greeted them.

"Am I glad to see you!" said Robinson Crusoe. "I've been shipwrecked here so long. It's very lonely!"

"Would you like to hear a story, Mr. Crusoe?"

"Would I ever!" he said.

Zack took the book and chose a story called *Gulliver's Travels*. As soon as he started reading, they could all hear a faint voice being carried by the wind.

"Help me! Help me!"

The voice was coming from a sailor named Gulliver. He was tied down to the ground by an army of tiny people called Lilliputians.

"Shoo, shoo," said Miss Smith. The Lilliputians scattered, and Miss Smith and her class helped untie the man.

"Thank you very much," said Gulliver. Then they noticed that the wind was picking up and blowing dark storms in their direction.

What to do now? Miss Smith thought. *I know!*

She picked up her *Incredible Storybook* and started reading a story called *Twenty Thousand Leagues Under the Sea*. The next moment the *Nautilus* submarine appeared by the shore.

The hatch opened, and Captain Nemo popped out.

"Can I be of assistance?" he asked. His voice could barely be heard above the roaring wind.

"Yes, a short trip in your submarine would be wonderful right now," Miss Smith shouted back.

"By all means! Welcome aboard," said Captain Nemo with a wave of his cap.

Once everyone was safely aboard, the *Nautilus* disappeared below the crashing waves into a quiet undersea world.

The submarine glided through the deep blue water. The view from the portholes was spectacular. Everywhere the class looked there were strange and colorful fish.

Captain Nemo gave a tour and explained everything they were seeing. "The *Nautilus* was built to study the world under the oceans and let people know how important it is to the earth." Just then, the *Nautilus* began to shake violently.

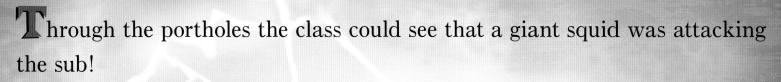

Through the portholes the class could see that a giant squid was attacking the sub!

It wrapped its tentacles around the *Nautilus* and lifted it right out of the water! It seemed as though the submarine would snap like a pretzel.

"Somebody *do* something!" screeched Sue-Ann.

"Full speed ahead!" said Zack, tugging Nemo's sleeve.

Captain Nemo cranked up the engines until they roared. The submarine could only inch forward, but the giant squid held on tight. Everyone closed their eyes—then finally, the giant squid lost its grip, and the sub shot up through the water. They were safe!

When the *Nautilus* surfaced, the storm was over, and the sun was setting. Miss Smith, the class, and the whole cast of storybook characters assembled on top.

"Well, it's been quite an exciting day, but it's getting late," said Miss Smith.
Then she finished reading the end of each story so all the characters could
go back into the *Incredible Storybook*. When she read the very last word,
quick as a flash, the class was back at the aquarium, heading for the bus.
Zack thought to himself, *I'll never look at the ocean the same way again.*

The Owl and the Pussycat are from the poem
"The Owl and the Pussycat" by Edward Lear (1871)

The Little Mermaid first appeared in the fairy tale
"The Little Mermaid" by Hans Christian Andersen (1837)

Captain Ahab and the White Whale are from
Moby Dick by Herman Melville (1851)

Captain Long John Silver and the Pirates are
from *Treasure Island* by Robert Louis Stevenson (1883)

Robinson Crusoe comes from the book
Robinson Crusoe by Daniel DeFoe (1719)

Gulliver and the Lilliputians are from
Gulliver's Travels by Jonathan Swift (1726)

Captain Nemo, the Nautilus, and the Giant Squid
come from *20,000 Leagues Under the Sea* by Jules Verne (1870)